SHAKESPEARE'S
STORYBOOK

For my parents, Mick and Fran — P. R.
For Max and Eloise, from your uncle — J. M.

Barefoot Books
2067 Massachusetts Ave
Cambridge, MA 02140

This book was typeset in Janson Text 12pt on 21pt leading
Illustrations were prepared in watercolor and pen and ink on watercolor paper
Graphic design by Penny Lamprell, Lymington
Color separation by Grafiscan, Verona
Printed and bound in China by Printplus, Ltd
This book has been printed on 100% acid-free paper

ISBN 978-1-84686-541-1

The Library of Congress Cataloging-in-Publication Data
can be found under LCCN 2001000237

1 3 5 7 9 8 6 4 2

SHAKESPEARE'S
STORYBOOK

Folk Tales that Inspired the Bard

Retold by

PATRICK RYAN

Illustrated by

JAMES MAYHEW

Barefoot Books
step inside a story

CONTENTS

INTRODUCTION

Astoryteller knows that a good story is worth telling more than once. And any storyteller can tell you that each time a tale is told, it may be a little different than it was before. Storytellers will also say that how a story is told depends on the listeners. An audience can affect a story in different ways, shaping it and changing it.

William Shakespeare was one of the best storytellers in the world. But he did not usually make up the stories that he told. He took popular stories and made them into poems and plays. He knew which stories his audiences would enjoy, so he wrote plays to please his listeners. He also used playwriting to express his own views about the world.

Shakespeare's audiences were familiar with the stories and poems that he based his plays upon. Today, most people know the stories only because they know the plays. But if you look at old books, and listen to storytellers who share tales in the traditional way, you will find other, older versions. Some of these stories are retold here.

Maybe Shakespeare heard these tales from his mother, or his grandfather, or his school teachers in Stratford-upon-Avon, where he grew up. Later, he and his players made their reputation at The Globe Theater, in London. Elizabeth I was queen, and during her reign the city became famous for its theaters and booksellers. People came to London from all over Europe; they brought tales from every corner of the world with them, and Shakespeare will have heard these stories, too.

So enjoy the stories in this book. As you read them, remember that there is no one standard version of each tale. Each of them has many sources which have changed from teller to teller. Shakespeare is just one more yarn spinner who belongs to this grand tradition.

Patrick Ryan

7

THE TAMING OF THE SHREW
The Devil's Bet

One of Shakespeare's earliest plays is *The Taming of the Shrew*, which he wrote in about 1592. The play tells of a young woman, named Katherina, who no one wants to marry because she has such a bad temper. Petruchio takes up the challenge. He also teaches her how to be kind so as to get what she wishes from life.

KATHERINA

Many folk tales are about the troubles husbands and wives have — their quarrels and the tricks they play on each other. In some versions, the husband torments the wife, and in others the wife torments the husband. Some stories suggest that being kind and thoughtful towards each other is a better route

PETRUCHIO

to lasting happiness than quarrelling and fighting. The most unusual version, retold here, involves a water demon who plays tricks on the wife because of her bad temper. The story comes from a number of sources, mostly Irish, some Welsh and some English. The Nicky Nicky Nye is actually found in Wales, and is a Gwent river spirit.

NICKY NICKY NYE

The main message of *The Taming of the Shrew*, that a "good match of equals" is important in marriage, is something that Shakespeare himself believed in. While he worked in London, his wife Anne raised their children and kept their business interests going in Stratford. She did so well that they were able to make as much money from her work as they did from Shakespeare's writing. It seems that in old age they did settle down to live happily together.

THE DEVIL'S BET

There was a widow who had a daughter named Nora. Nora was beautiful, but very grumpy and terribly lazy. She never lifted a finger to help and never had a kind word. Spoiled and quarrelsome, Nora always had her own way.

In the forest nearby lived a woodsman called Jamie. He had a comfortable, pretty cottage and wanted someone to share it with. There was just one problem. In the spring by his home dwelt the Nicky Nicky Nye, a wicked water devil. This did not worry Jamie, for the devil only came out at night. And why should it worry his wife-to-be? What bother is a demon if a woodsman and his wife each have a good strong spirit?

Jamie saddled his donkey and went in search of a wife — a sparky young woman he could fall in love with. He hadn't gone far when he came upon the widow's daughter.

Nora was sitting by the river, dirty laundry scattered all about her. Her mother had sent her to do the washing. Instead she sat and daydreamed, while the clothes drifted in the tide.

Jamie asked a passing farmer, "Who is that beauty, and has she a sweetheart?"

"That's Nora!" laughed the farmer. "Nasty Nora they call her. No one could ever love her."

"I could," declared the woodsman. "With all my heart."

"Well, good luck," the farmer replied. "She's so contrary she gives her poor mother nothing but grief. The widow tries to keep things tidy, but Nora always makes a mess."

"All the more reason to marry me!" smiled Jamie. "She can come to live in my pretty cottage. Tidy or messy, I don't mind." He began to move away.

"Hang on — I've more to tell you!" continued the farmer. "Her mother sent Nora to buy food for supper, and the selfish girl spent the money on ribbons for her hair!"

"So, a woman who needs little," laughed Jamie. "All the better for me — and what pretty hair to tie up with ribbons!"

So saying, he went up to Nora and said ever so politely, "Pretty maiden, your fine clothes will soon be washed away in the tide. Permit me to help fetch them back."

"Do what you like!" sniffed Nora.

"Very well," laughed Jamie. "I'll be glad to help."

With that he picked Nora up — which she liked very much for he was a strong handsome fellow. Then he threw her in the river — which she didn't like at all.

"There you go!" he cried. "You'll catch the clothes easily enough, now you're in the water!"

Spluttering and swearing, gasping and moaning, Nora gathered up the garments and stomped back to the bank.

"And you needn't mind about getting wet," Jamie told her. "The water will wash away all your grumpiness."

Cursing and raging, she threw the wet things in Jamie's face.

"Whoa, Nora," cried Jamie. "Is that how to treat your sweetheart?"

"What sweetheart?" shrieked Nora. "I'll never be sweet to you!"

"Oh, but you will," Jamie promised. "You and I are getting married today!"

With that, he took Nora by the arm and escorted

her to her mother. The widow looked so tired and sad that Jamie resolved to marry Nora at once. Then the mother would be able to live in peace, and perhaps learn to smile again.

Jamie sat down and told them of his cottage in the wood, and the garden all around with songbirds singing and bees humming. It all sounded so lovely, for he made no mention of the water devil lurking in the well. Nora agreed she was tired of living with her mother. She fancied life in a pretty cottage of her own, especially with a handsome husband like Jamie with his curly black hair. True, he had played a trick on her — but couldn't she play tricks too? They might be well matched.

So they went to the church to get married. Jamie and the widow were in such a hurry, Nora had no time to change out of her wet clothes. She had no time to celebrate either, for Jamie whisked her away straight after the wedding.

"We must hurry and get back before dark," Jamie explained, as they trotted along on the donkey into the thick dark wood. He wanted to be indoors before the demon showed itself.

"This donkey's too slow, too lumpy, too bumpy to move quickly," grumbled Nora. "Why don't you beat him with your stick?"

"Beat my dear donkey?" exclaimed Jamie. "No, no, no, that would never do."

"Why not?" asked Nora. "It would make him go faster."

Jamie only replied, "I have found, my dear, that soft words and a gentle touch win more than harsh words and mean tricks."

As night fell, they came to the pretty cottage.

Jamie's dog rushed out to greet them, barking and jumping for joy, and splattering them with mud from head to toe.

"The dirty beast!" screamed Nora. "That dog's too loud, his paws are too muddy, his tongue's too wet! Why don't you beat him with your stick?"

"Beat my dear doggie?" exclaimed Jamie. "No, no, no, that would never do."

"Why not?" asked Nora. "It would make him behave."

But Jamie only replied, "I have found, my dear, that soft words and a gentle touch win more than harsh words and mean tricks."

Then he opened the door of the cottage, and in they went.

"Nora, dear darling, I'm so thirsty," said Jamie as they stepped inside. "Please make us a pot of tea while I fetch more wood for the fire."

"I'm not your servant!" snapped Nora, her eyes blazing. "And here's to your pot of tea!"

With these cross words, she smashed the china teapot on the floor, adding cheekily, "Where do soft words and a gentle touch get you now?"

"I suppose I deserved that for dropping you in the river," said Jamie. "But your harsh words and mean tricks have hurt you as much as me. Without a teapot, there'll be no tea for either of us!"

Before Nora could reply, there was a rumble of laughter from the well. Up out of the water jumped the demon, and through the window popped the head of the Nicky Nicky Nye.

"Ho, ho, ho," he laughed. "Jamie, who have you there?"

"My wife, Nora," Jamie answered proudly.

"A wife!" roared the devil. "She'll not stay long — not with me about!"

"Who says I'll not stay?" shouted Nora.

"I do!" snapped the demon. "The Nicky Nicky Nye! You'll not last a week with me around."

"I bet I will!" snarled Nora, gritting her teeth. "No one chases me away."

"Right," said the Nicky Nicky Nye. "The bet's on. I'll bet all the gold and silver hidden in my well that I can drive you away before the week is out!"

"Done," said Nora. "But it's you who'll be going."

"We'll see!" grinned the water devil. "And if you lose the bet — I'll gobble you up as you try to run away!"

Then the Nicky Nicky Nye sank back into the well, and Jamie's smiling face turned glum.

"Oh dear, dear," he said. "Nora, what have you done? I don't want the Nicky Nicky Nye to gobble you up."

"He won't! I'll see to him!" said Nora determinedly.

"Just remember," begged her husband, "soft words and a gentle touch win more than mean tricks."

Between Nora and the demon it was war. The water devil only came out at night, but Nora couldn't escape him. Every time she entered the garden, the Nicky Nicky Nye would throw at her the foulest stuff from nearby ponds and streams — scum and duckweed, mud and sludge. Dripping with slime, Nora would try to get her own back by dumping the dirty dishwater into the well, or emptying the chamber pot onto the demon's head. But he only spat it back in her face.

It went on like this each day until, finally, Nora could bear it no more. She no longer cared for the pretty cottage or even her handsome black-haired husband. She just wanted to run away — then remembered that, if she did, the Nicky Nicky Nye would gobble her up.

"Harsh words and mean tricks won't win," Jamie reminded her. "Soft words and a gentle touch are what do the job best."

The last night had arrived and Nora was all ready to flee. But Jamie's advice came back to her and at last gave her an idea. She packed a basket of food, as if ready to leave, then came to stand by the well.

"Ha ha!" laughed the demon when he saw her. "I've won the bet! You're running away — get ready to be gobbled up!"

"You're quite wrong, my darling little demon," Nora smiled.

"I'm not running away. It's such a lovely day I thought I'd go for a stroll in the garden."

"You're mad!" said the water devil. "It's the middle of the night."

"No," disagreed Nora. "Just look at the bright blinding sun!"

"That's the moon!" roared the devil.

"No, it's the sun," grinned Nora. "And I'm so worried to see you out and about in the daylight."

"It's not daylight!" shouted the water devil. "It's moonlight!"

Nora ignored him. "And you never come out

in the day, only in the night. I fear you may soon shrivel up!"

"I don't need your concern," grumbled the Nicky Nicky Nye. "So I made you some sweet refreshing lemonade," said Nora, as she opened the basket and brought out a bottle.

"I hate lemonade!" shouted the devil. "Leave me alone!"

But Nora would not let the demon be. She smothered him with kindness. She charmed him with soft words, and plied him with lemonade and cakes, biscuits and sweets. The Nicky Nicky Nye could not bear it.

"I think I'm going to be sick!" he cried.

"There, there," Nora soothed. "As my husband says, a soft word and a gentle touch will take care of that."

And she gave the Nicky Nicky Nye a pat on the head. The monster was so overcome by all this kindness that he truly could not bear it. He huffed and puffed and blew himself up bigger and bigger and bigger — until he burst.

And that was the end of the Nicky Nicky Nye. Never again did he bother the woodsman and his wife. Deep down at the bottom of the well Jamie and Nora found the Nicky Nicky Nye's hoard of gold and silver, which they kept for themselves. Nora had won the devil's bet, after all. From that time on she and Jamie tried to get by as best they could — with soft words and a gentle touch.

ROMEO AND JULIET
The Hill of Roses

The tale of Romeo and Juliet is one of the best-known love stories in the world. It is one of Shakespeare's most popular plays, and one of his first tragedies. The play, written in 1595, tells of two young people who live in Verona, a town in Italy. Their families hate each other, but when Romeo and Juliet fall in love, they defy their parents and get married secretly. It is not until the young lovers die that the two families finally agree to get along together.

Many versions of the tale of Romeo and Juliet existed before Shakespeare made the story into a play. The story retold here draws upon a love story by Bernard Garter, *The Tragicall and True Historie which Happened between Two English Lovers* (1563), and on an ancient Scottish folk tale, "The Stone of Roses."

ROMEO

But its main source is *Il Novellino* by Masuccio Salernitano (1474), one of the oldest written accounts of the love story, and one which Shakespeare, too, may have known.

Many people believe that the story of Romeo and Juliet is in fact a true tale of two feuding families from medieval Verona. There were, long ago in that part of Italy, people with the same surnames as those of the lovers' two families. To this day, people go to Verona to visit the house that is thought to have belonged to Juliet's family. You can even see the balcony where Romeo was supposed to have courted Juliet!

Juliet

THE HILL OF ROSES

Far away in a distant land there rises a hill completely covered with roses. There is an old story of how the hill came to be that way, but it is hardly ever told. Some say it's a tale too sad for the telling.

In ancient times, two villages stood on either side of that hill. The people of each village were sworn enemies. They would have nothing to do with each other, and there was no business between them. When troubled times came, the villagers of one hamlet refused to help those of the other. When good times returned, the two villages never celebrated together. There was never any love between the two villages, only hatred.

The hill that separated these hamlets became a kind of no man's land. In time it became the only thing the villages shared, for both used the hill as a graveyard for their dead.

Now in one village there lived a man called Romeus. He was young and reckless. Some called him brave, others said he was crazy. He was always doing wild things to show off to his friends.

In the other village was a young woman named Julietta, who lived with Tibbot, her brother.

"Julietta's the most beautiful girl in the world!" That's what everyone claimed. Even the people in Romeus' village had to admit she was lovely.

So one midwinter, when Julietta and Tibbot's father announced he would be hosting a fancy dress ball, everyone wanted to go. Even the men of Romeus's village, who were enemies of Julietta's people, wanted to go so they could see her. But no one dared.

"How I wish I could take a look at this Julietta!" sighed Quicksilver, Romeus's best friend.

"I'll go and look at her," boasted Romeus. "After all, who's to know? The party is fancy dress!"

"Then I dare you!" Quicksilver teased, never dreaming that Romeus would.

The crazy boy disguised himself, dressing up as a nymph so no one would recognize him. Carefully climbing the hill, he found his way down the path that wound into Julietta's village, and slipped into the ballroom. At the first chance, he grabbed Julietta's arm and swept her into a dance. His hands felt warm, while everyone else's had been freezing!

"Thank you for the dance," smiled Julietta as she curtsied to him. "And for giving me your warm hands — for they've warmed mine."

It was then they looked into each other's eyes, and fell in love. When Romeus left the ball, Julietta followed him. She paused when she saw him entering the graveyard to climb the hill. Could she have fallen in love with a ghost? Even so, that love made her follow Romeus up the path. Seeing him head down the other side of the hill, she realized he came from the village of her enemies. Even so, she called, "Wait, please, wait!"

Romeus stopped. When he turned and saw Julietta, he hurried back to her, took her by the hand again, and they kissed. For a long while they stood in the cold winter's moonlight talking and talking, as if they would never stop. When at last they parted, they had planned to meet again.

"Whenever we can and wish to meet, let us send one another a rose," said Julietta. And Romeus agreed.

So it was that each week, sometimes each day, Romeus would send a red rose plucked from the glasshouse in his garden, or Julietta a white rose carefully cultivated in the sheltered cloisters of her village church. That was a sign that one of them would be at the top of the hill in the evening. And the other would always be there, with a warm welcome.

Their love grew. But they dared not tell anyone about it, even family or friends. Romeus and Julietta hoped they might get married, and so bring their

people together. As winter passed and songbirds began to return to welcome in the spring, they promised each other that soon they would find a way to wed.

Time passed, and the people of each village grew to hate each other more than ever. Many feared the two places would each be destroyed, and everyone killed. Tibbot, Julietta's own brother, was one of those most full of hate. He was ever watchful, always looking for signs of his enemies and itching to pick a fight. It wasn't long before he became suspicious of Julietta's quiet but secret ways. He began to follow her, suspecting that his own sister had betrayed him and his friends by falling in love with one of the enemy.

One spring night, as Romeus and Julietta walked arm in arm atop the hill, the snow began to fall. So cold and heavy was the unseasonable blizzard that Romeus begged Julietta to let him take her safely back to her house, where he would spend the night, or to return with him to his home.

"We can't do that!" gasped Julietta. "We can't spend the night together under one roof until we're married."

"Then let's marry tonight!" Romeus pleaded. Julietta looked into his eyes and agreed at once.

They raced through the snow to the little church by the graveyard, and knocked loudly at the door to wake the friar. This holy man had long prayed that the villages would stop their fighting. When he had listened to the young people and learned of their eagerness to be wed, he agreed to marry them — for he hoped that this would put an end to the quarrel.

That night was the happiest Romeus and Julietta had ever known. They woke, in Julietta's house, to the sound of a nightingale singing in harmony with the lark. The snowstorm of the night before had melted away, and Romeus carefully made his way home. That day each would tell their fellow villagers of the marriage that had taken place. If the people would not join together to celebrate their happiness, then he and Julietta would run away together to make a new life somewhere else.

But it was too late. As Romeus approached his village, he found it under attack. Julietta's brother, Tibbot, had seen them on the hill the night before, and now knew for certain that his sister loved one of the enemy. In his fury he had led a gang of angry young men around the hill to burn down the neighboring village. He wanted to destroy it completely and save his sister from her folly. But Quicksilver, always on the lookout for trouble, had seen Tibbot and his men approach with flaming torches in their hands. He roused his people at once to fight the gang and save their homes.

This was the mad scene that greeted Romeus as he entered his village. He ran at once into the fray. "Stop!" he screamed. "Stop the fighting!"

Just at that moment, Quicksilver dashed at Tibbot with his sword. Romeus pushed his friend away, so as to save the brother of his wife. But Tibbot was too quick: as Quicksilver fell, Tibbot stabbed him with his dagger, killing him at once.

"Murderer!" cried Romeus, mad with grief. Seizing Quicksilver's sword, he lunged at Tibbot. Single-handedly, he drove out Tibbot and all his men, sending them back to their village.

Back at home, Tibbot told his sister the grim news, watching her to see what she would do.

Julietta wept with fear. "And how was Romeus, when you left him?" she begged to know.

"You snake-in-the-grass!" roared Tibbot. "You do love him!"

"We were married last night," Julietta admitted through her tears. "He's my husband now."

"Never," spat Tibbot. "You're lying! You'll never be married to him! You'll marry a man of this village — you'll marry who I say! You will marry the first man I bring back to this house!"

34

With that, Tibbot went out to fetch a man, any man, to force on his beautiful sister, whom he now hated more than anything in the world.

Julietta ran at once to the friar and told him of all the disasters that had occurred. "What am I to do?" she cried. "I can't get to Romeus in time, and I dare not stay with my brother!"

"First, we must try to calm everyone down," replied the friar. "When all is quiet, then everything can be sorted out. We must try to make peace."

"But how?" Julietta implored. "The only peace these villages know is the peace that comes with death."

This gave the friar his plan.

He told Julietta of a certain potion. If taken, this potion would make a person appear to be dead when, truly, he only slept a very deep sleep from which he would awaken after three days.

35

"Let me drink this potion!" Julietta insisted. "When Tibbot thinks I'm dead, my people will bury me. You then can make the peace. If you cannot, send a white rose to my husband with a message that he is to meet me at my tomb, and take me away to a place where we can love each other in freedom."

The friar agreed to all this. Julietta drank the potion and collapsed to the floor of the church. The priest raised the alarm, and when Tibbot came he was told the news.

"You see what you have done?" said the friar with great sadness. "Your beautiful sister has died of a broken heart."

There was much weeping and wailing then. Tibbot ordered that all fighting should cease for a while, out of respect for his sister. A funeral was arranged, and a grand tomb built, and Julietta was placed within.

Throughout the funeral, the friar begged Tibbot to make peace. But Tibbot refused, promising instead, "When my sister's buried, we'll destroy those who broke her heart!"

So the friar had no choice but to pluck a white rose from the church cloister and tie to it a message for Romeus:

Your true love is not dead ~ She waits for you and wishes a new life for you both. Meet her at her tomb.

This was sent at once to Romeus. That night he eagerly climbed the hill to meet his love. But guarding the tomb was Tibbot, who rushed at Romeus with his sword. At once the two of them were fighting, tooth and nail. But Tibbot's grief made him stronger, and before long Romeus fell to the ground — dead.

At that moment, the tomb opened and Julietta, now awake, stepped out. At the sight of her husband lying dead at Tibbot's feet, she flew at her brother, crying, "You've killed him! You've killed him! For this you'll pay dearly!"

Tibbot went pale with shock and almost fainted.

He had believed his sister dead, and thought this must be her ghost come back to haunt him.

"Julietta, forgive me!" he begged, falling to his knees. "Tell me what to do so you won't curse me!"

"Make peace between the villages," Julietta commanded. "And never try to see me again."

Shaking with fear, Tibbot turned and fled. Never truly understanding what had happened, but fearing his sister whether dead or alive, he made sure that peace between the villages came at last.

Romeus was buried by his friends in the grave meant for Julietta. Julietta remained in the tomb with her dead husband. She would not leave, longing only for death herself.

The friar, horrified at how everything had gone so wrong, pleaded with Julietta to leave the graveyard and live again among her people. But she refused. She made the tomb a holy place, where she lived as a hermit. And not long after the death of her beloved Romeus, she died of a broken heart. The friar placed her in the tomb, beside Romeus.

The sad story of what had happened was told throughout the land. Everyone came to know the tale. Many people whose hearts had been ruined by love came to see the place for themselves. From that time on, the people of both villages planted roses on that hill: red ones and white ones. Roses in memory of those who had died for love. Roses to remind the villagers of the true cost of hatred, and the price of peace. And even to this day the hill is covered with roses — red blooms all mingled with white.

The Merchant of Venice
A Bargain is a Bargain

The *Merchant of Venice* (1596 – 1598), is about a young man called Antonio, who borrows money from a Jewish money lender, Shylock. He does this to help his friend Bassanio marry the wise and beautiful Portia. Later, Shylock's daughter runs away to marry a Christian. Shylock is so angry that when Antonio does not repay his debt, he insists that he pay with a pound of flesh. Portia helps to resolve this terrible dilemma.

In choosing a Jewish merchant, Shakespeare may have had in mind a couple of incidents, supposedly true, that happened in his time. The first concerned a Jewish merchant in Italy who lost a bet with a bishop friend of his, and might have had to pay with a pound of flesh if the Pope had not come to his rescue. In Shakespeare's day, the

SHYLOCK

Christian church did not permit Christians to lend money. So it was one business that Jews could run — but they were not very popular for providing this service.

PORTIA

The second incident also concerns a Jew. Elizabeth I had a doctor named Lopez, a Portuguese Jew, who refused to help the Earl of Essex in his plot to betray the queen. The earl was so popular that people believed him when he said Lopez had tried to poison the queen, so the loyal doctor was hanged for treason. Shakespeare might well have known Dr. Lopez. He almost certainly knew what the earl had done, for the Earl of Essex even attempted to get Shakespeare's theater company to help in his plot to destroy the queen. Eventually the earl was caught and punished. It is quite likely that Shakespeare mixed these incidents with the folk tales to make his famous play.

ANTONIO

A Bargain is a Bargain

There was once a rich merchant who had two sons. These brothers were as different as the crow and the peacock, or as the moon and the sun, or as hot and cold. The elder, serious and somber, cared only for money. The younger was friendly and warm, always joking and often foolish.

Their old father was ill. He knew his time had come and called his sons to his side. "My boys," said the merchant, "I'm close to death. All my life I have worked hard, built a business, made a fortune. I leave all that to you. Now tell me, what will you each do with my money?"

The older son promised to use his inheritance wisely and keep the family business going.

But did the younger boy say, "Father, I'm going to be just like you — a great businessman"? No, he did not. Instead he said, "Father, I'm going to spend your money! I'm going to have a good time! I'll buy fancy clothes, good food and wine. I'll have music, and dancing, and beautiful women around me always!"

These words broke his father's heart, and the old man died in that instant.

The older brother became ever more serious, and wisely invested the fortune left to him. Soon, he was even more successful than his father had been.

And the younger brother did just as he had promised. He went on a spree. He dressed in expensive clothes of the latest fashion. He flirted with young women, and hired musicians so as to hear sweet melodies all the time. He didn't even think about work. He feasted on the finest food, drank the best wine and held wild parties.

Soon he had spent all his fortune. Penniless, he found his friends soon left him. They were the kind who only stick with someone who has money. The young man was homeless, dressed

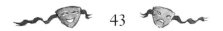

in rags. Living in the street, he became a beggar. People said it was shameful. The older brother was disgusted with his younger brother. But the young man didn't mind being poor. He seemed perfectly happy.

Now, the duke of that city had a daughter who was both beautiful and wise. Many men asked for her hand. But she had no desire to wed, for she loved only books and stories, thoughts and ideas. She turned all of her suitors down and spent her days reading.

Even so, men pestered her, and the duke demanded she choose a husband. So his daughter devised a test. She gave orders for three caskets to be made: the first of gold, the second of silver, and the last of wood. She declared that if any man could solve the puzzle and choose the casket that held the prize worth having, he would be her husband. Many tried to solve the puzzle, but all failed.

So the duke's daughter happily continued her peaceful existence — absorbed in her books. The only distractions that could tempt her away from the palace, and her beloved books, were the fun-filled festivals and lively carnivals for which her city was famed.

One day, when carnival was in full swing, the younger brother caught sight of the duke's daughter. He fell in love with her at once, and was determined to solve the puzzle and marry her.

But how could he appear before her in rags? Could a beggar marry the daughter of a duke? It seemed impossible, but this young man was full of cheek. He went to his brother and asked for some money.

"Why should I give money to you, you young scoundrel?" grumbled the older brother.

"Because, dear brother," the younger man lied,

"I'm so sorry for my foolishness and wickedness. I want to make amends. I want to be like you and father. Give me some money, so I can prove myself and be a merchant."

His brother didn't believe him. He wouldn't part with any of his money, not a single penny.

"Then loan me the money, brother!" he pleaded. "With the carnival on, I can sell many things. I'm sure to make a great fortune!"

"What if you fail and can't pay me back?" asked the older brother.

"If I can't pay with money," the younger one swore, "I'll pay with anything you want — just name it!"

"You've nothing! Nothing but your own flesh!" exclaimed his exasperated brother.

"Then I'll pay with that," he announced. "If I can't pay with money, I shall pay with my own flesh."

"Very well," agreed his brother. "I'll

 47

loan the amount you ask for. If you can't pay me back by the end of carnival, then I'll cut away a pound of flesh from the place closest to your heart."

A bargain was made, a deal done, an agreement settled upon. Documents were drawn up and the contract signed and witnessed. The younger brother took the money, never dreaming he would have to pay it back. "My brother will be so proud when I'm married to the duke's daughter, he'll not care about the money," he thought to himself.

Certainly he never believed that his brother would cut away a pound of his flesh — that was just a jest. But the brother was deadly serious, and determined to punish the younger man, if necessary, to teach him a lesson.

Rather than spend the money on goods to sell at carnival, the young man had the finest clothes made up. Dressed in the latest fashion, he cut a fine figure. One would have thought he was a prince, or even an emperor. He went to the palace and demanded that the duke's daughter put him to the test.

The young man was taken at once to her chamber, where the three caskets sat. He was asked to choose the one that held the prize worth having. Carefully he read the inscription on each casket.

The golden casket read: "Who chooses me shall find what everyone becomes in the end."

"I don't want that one," said the young man. "For not everyone becomes the husband of a duke's daughter."

The golden casket was opened, and it was full of dust and bones.

The silver casket said: "Who chooses me shall find what everyone gets in the end."

"No, take it away," ordered the youth. "For not everyone gets the daughter of a duke."

The silver casket was opened. Inside, it was full of moldy soil and wriggling worms.

The wooden casket had written on it: "Who chooses me finds what goodness grants."

"That's the one I want!" he declared. The wooden box was opened, and inside was a gorgeous golden ring set with diamonds and pearls.

"Well chosen," observed the duke's daughter, not without a little sigh. "So is that the prize worth having?"

"No," said the young man, "the prize is not this ring. The reward is to marry you — for is this not our engagement ring?"

"It is," the duke's daughter agreed — rather sadly. "You've solved the puzzle. We shall be married. Wear that ring always, for it is a token of the bond between us. Never part with it, or our wedding will not take place."

Proudly the young man put the ring upon his finger. Then away he went to celebrate his success. With money left from his brother's loan, he bought food and wine. Soon his old friends were back and a grand time was had by all. By the time carnival had ended, all the money was spent.

With carnival over, the older brother sought the young man and demanded his money back. His brother laughed and said, "I've nothing to pay you with today — all the money is gone. But wait just a little longer, for soon I'll be marrying the duke's daughter and will pay you ten times what I owe!"

"Scallywag! No daughter of a duke will marry you!" roared the brother. "Pay my money now, or I cut out a pound of your flesh this very day!"

The young man realized with horror that his brother was deadly serious. He pleaded for mercy, but the older brother insisted on his pound of flesh. The youth was thrown into prison, so the matter could be judged.

"Let the duke solve this — I know he'll favor me!" boasted the older brother. "A bargain is a bargain, a contract is a contract, a deal is a deal. You signed the papers, you must pay with your flesh!"

Weeping and wailing, the younger brother paced his prison cell, thinking desperately what he could do to save himself. Then an idea came to him. He wrote a message and had the guard take it to the duke's daughter. She read it and came at once.

"Husband-to-be, how did you get thrown into my father's dungeons?" she asked. The young man told his story, of his recklessness with money and the conditions of the loan.

"This is bad, this is very bad," said the duke's daughter with a sigh. "You were foolish to put your life at risk, but it's also wicked for your brother to behave in this way. When you come to my father's court, you must have the best lawyer!"

"But lawyers cost money!" cried the young man. "And I have none."

"Never worry," smiled the duke's daughter. "I'll see to it that you have a lawyer."

When the day came for the brothers to argue their case before the duke, his daughter dismissed all her servants. She cut off her hair and removed

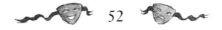

her beautiful gown of satin and lace. Instead she put on the dusky robes of a lawyer. Dressed like this, she passed easily for a man.

No one knew her as she entered the courtroom and declared herself to be the young man's advocate. The case was called, the brothers stepped forward.

The story was told to the duke, who looked over the documents and asked, "Is all this true?"

The young man admitted it was. The duke frowned. "I don't like this case, this bad feeling between brothers. But it seems your brother has the right to cut away your flesh. Before I decide, what does the law say?"

The duke's daughter rose and proclaimed, "Your worship, the law says a bargain is a bargain, an agreement is an agreement, a contract is a contract, a deal is a deal. This young man borrowed the money, and can't pay it back. He agreed to give a pound of flesh instead, so his brother has the right to cut away that flesh this very instant."

The young man didn't much like the words of his lawyer. Then she went on, for lawyers do talk a lot.

"However," she said, "because a bargain is a bargain, an agreement is an agreement, a contract is a contract, a deal is a deal, it must be honored to the letter. The bargain was that exactly and precisely one pound of flesh be cut. So his brother must take no more and no less than a pound of flesh. If he cuts an ounce more or less than a pound, then he must give all his money to the city for breaking his word."

Now it was the older brother who was unhappy, but still the lawyer talked on.

"Furthermore," she declared, "the law says no person may spill the blood of another. If blood is spilled, then the older brother must have his head chopped off in punishment. So let exactly, precisely one pound of flesh be cut without a drop of blood spilled, or the older brother loses his money and his head. That is what the law says!"

"Excellent," cried the duke. "A brilliant reading of the law! You're the finest lawyer ever to speak in my court." Then he turned to the older brother: "Sir, take your pound of flesh without any blood, but break the law and you are ruined."

The older brother went away furious, with neither his money nor his pound of flesh. The younger brother was about to dash away to the duke's daughter to tell her the good news, when his lawyer stopped him.

"Sir, before you go, you must pay your lawyer," she declared.

"But I've no money," he croaked. "You know that. Just wait a little and my beloved will give me money to pay you."

"That won't do," said the duke's daughter, frowning. "You're a reckless young man, and I think not to be trusted. That ring on your finger — give it to me."

"I cannot!" the young man protested. "It was given to me by the duke's daughter. I promised never to remove it."

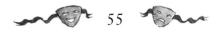

"Give it to me now," she commanded. "I shall hold it until you return with money to pay me."

Reluctantly, the young man gave her the ring. Then he dashed from the courtroom.

But the duke's daughter was quicker, and changed out of her clothes at once so he would not recognize her as his lawyer.

"My beloved, I'm saved!" he shouted as he raced up to her. "Now we can be married."

"That we cannot be," the duke's daughter calmly replied. "Look at your hand. Already you've lost the ring I made you promise to keep."

"But I had to pay the lawyer!" wailed the young man. "I had nothing else to give him."

"To pay a mere lawyer you gave up the prize worth having!" exclaimed the duke's daughter. "I think your love for me is too little. The bond between us is now broken — you'll not be my husband now!"

Both brothers were now disappointed in their fortunes. The younger one returned to the streets.

A beggar once again, perhaps he was still happy-go-lucky, or maybe what had happened had made him wiser and more serious.

Meanwhile, the duke's daughter settled down happily with her books — pleased that she had saved two brothers from their wickedness and foolishness, but gladder still that it was she who had won a prize worth having.

As You Like It
Snowdrop

A*s You Like It* (late 1590s) is based on a book called *Rosalynde* by Thomas Lodge. Like the book, the play tells of some young people whose families do not get along well. One uncle takes the dukedom from his brother, the rightful ruler. The rightful duke and his friends hide in the forest as outlaws. The duke's daughter, Rosalind, stays at court to keep her cousin company. Both girls fall in love — with brothers who fight like the father and uncle. When her uncle banishes her, Rosalind dresses as a boy and escapes with her cousin to live in the woods. There they join the outlaws, who turn out to be their old friends and relations. Soon, all the lovers get together and the rightful duke is given back his dukedom.

Like Lodge, Shakespeare set his story in France. But the forest in

ROSALIND

As You Like It is like an English forest. In fact, it is like the forest that was once around Warwick Castle, near Stratford-upon-Avon. Shakespeare also mentions Robin Hood and his Merry Men in this play and says his characters are just like those old heroes. Like Lodge, he too may have been inspired by early versions of "Snow White," also known as "Snowdrop." In these versions, the heroine lives with friendly robbers, not with dwarves.

The idea of a woman disguised as a man and living with outlaws was also popular — indeed, Shakespeare used it in two more plays, *Cymbeline* and *Twelfth Night*. It may be that he combined the fairy tale, the legend of Robin Hood, and Lodge's book to create a play full of the things that audiences enjoy. This is how the play gets its name — for it is written to be just as you (the audience) like it.

SNOWDROP

In a time before yours or mine, there was a queen who had a daughter. She called her Snowdrop, for the girl was as beautiful as the flowers of spring. The queen cared for Snowdrop more than anything in the world. Because of this, she neglected her duties and lost the kingdom to a man who was both clever and wicked. He banished the queen and made himself king, but he kept Snowdrop as a slave, to do all the work in the palace.

This new king was hard and cruel. His only joy was his son, a merry lad named Will. The king wished to raise his boy to be just like him.

But Will was not like his father, and cared nothing about ruling the kingdom. So, in spite of everything, Snowdrop and Will became the best of playmates and loved each other dearly.

The people in the kingdom were not happy with their harsh new ruler. They looked at Snowdrop and saw her goodness. They talked of how sweet and fair she was. They said the former princess should one day be their ruler, not Will, and certainly not his wicked father.

The king heard this and was furious. His hatred for Snowdrop grew until at last he couldn't bear the sight of her. In secret, the king ordered his most trusted servant to take Snowdrop to the forest and kill her.

Snowdrop overheard this plan, but she wasn't frightened. That night she packed a few things, kissed her playmate goodbye and ran into the forest to seek her own way in life.

She wandered around the forest until she was so tired and hungry she could go no further. It was then that she stumbled upon a cave. Stepping inside, she found the cave was like the finest palace, full of sparkling treasure.

"This is some robbers' den!" Snowdrop cried.

"I've got to get out of here!"

Just as she was about to leave, she noticed a table in the middle of the cave — all laid out with the robbers' supper. The table was piled high with good things: cakes, pastries and all kinds of sweets!

Snowdrop was so famished that she stopped to take a bite from each dish and a sip from each goblet. She got ready to leave once again, but it was too late. Clomp, clomp came the sound of the robbers' feet. They were returning for their supper! Quick as a flash, Snowdrop jumped into a cupboard and closed the door behind her.

The three robbers, all brothers, saw at once someone had taken their food. Angrily they looked for this thief who had dared rob them. Then the youngest discovered Snowdrop, shaking with fear in the cupboard.

"Brothers, I've found the thief! Not a bad catch too!" he bragged.

"Grind his bones! Boil his blood! Mash his flesh!" ordered the older two robbers.

But when they saw
Snowdrop, looking so
sweet and gentle, they
knew they couldn't harm her.
Instead, they let her stay with
them, promising to love and
protect her as they would
each other.

This was how Snowdrop became one of the robbers. She dressed as a man, and helped them with their work. They stole from the rich and used the money to help the weak and poor who suffered under the cruel king.

One day Snowdrop met up with her old playmate, Will. It came about this way.

Will was so lonely that he wandered into the woods each day, hoping to find Snowdrop. He even wrote poems in her honor, and hung them on every tree for her to find them. By following these love letters, Snowdrop finally tracked down Will.

Will didn't recognize her at first. When he did,

he hugged her close and begged her to return with him to the palace. Snowdrop had to refuse.

"Please don't be sad," she said. "We've found each other again. And I'll see you every day — as long as you promise to stop writing those silly poems and hanging them on the trees! A robber can't have poetry written about her!"

Will promised. They met each day in a grove of apple trees and were wonderfully happy once again.

But the king noticed his son's changed mood. He saw how happy Will was whenever he returned from the forest, and grew suspicious. So one day he

followed his son to the apple grove, where he saw Will meeting Snowdrop. Seeing that the girl was still alive, his hatred grew stronger than ever and he resolved to get rid of Snowdrop once and for all.

Not long after that, the king disguised himself as a peddler woman. With a basket full of delights and dainties, he made his way into the forest, until he came to the robbers' cave. He knocked briskly upon the door of the cave, and Snowdrop answered.

"Good day, old woman," said Snowdrop. She did not recognize the king.

"Good day to you, my darling," croaked the king.

"Would you like some trinkets from my basket?"

Now, the basket was full of baubles and laces and ribbons that caught the eye. One necklace shone brighter than the rest, and it so pleased Snowdrop that she bought it at once. The king offered to fasten it around the girl's neck, pulling the necklace so tight that it strangled Snowdrop and she fell to the ground. The evil king ran off, leaving her to die.

But Snowdrop's robber brothers returned to find her, and they loosened the necklace. They rubbed her hands and her face with vinegar and sugar water. Slowly the color came back to her cheeks, and she opened her eyes.

"Never, ever open that door when you're here alone!" the robbers made her promise.

Later, when the king followed Will to the apple grove, he saw that his trick had been of no use. But his wickedness was such he could not give up trying to destroy the girl. This time he made himself up as a flower seller, and with a basket of flowers he went back to the cave in the woods.

The king knocked, and sweetly talked, but Snowdrop wouldn't let him in, nor would she come out. So he left a bunch of poisoned flowers at the door, saying they were a gift to show he meant no harm. When the robbers returned, Snowdrop fetched the flowers and threw them straight on the fire. A terrible stink of poisonous fumes arose with the smoke.

"Never again," Snowdrop vowed, "do I speak to any old peddler women! I'm sure they've been sent by the king to destroy me."

The king soon learned that Snowdrop still lived. He knew Snowdrop and Will continued to meet and that they loved each other more than ever.

So he filled a basket with poisoned apples and malignant pears. These he took to the grove where Will and Snowdrop met each day. He dropped the poisoned apples and pears all around that orchard. Then the king hid behind a tree, to be sure his plan worked and so he could see that Snowdrop was destroyed.

Soon Snowdrop came and waited for her friend. Seeing the apples lying on the ground, so pretty and red, she couldn't resist them. She picked one up, took a bite, and fell down dead.

Full of glee, the king returned to the palace.

It was the robbers who found Snowdrop. They wept and cried, but this time they could not awaken her. So they fashioned a glass coffin for her to rest in. So beautiful was she, even in death, that they could not bear to place her under the ground. Instead, they captured a wild horse and strapped the coffin to its back. They let the horse go — to wander through the land carrying Snowdrop in her glass coffin so that all could gaze upon her beauty.

When Will came back to the apple grove the next day, Snowdrop was not there.

He waited but she did not come. Again his heart was broken from loneliness. He wandered for many days, looking for his beloved Snowdrop. Then at last he returned to the palace.

Word soon spread about the mysterious horse

that carried a beautiful maiden, sleeping in a glass box. Many tried to catch a glimpse of this strange sight. Some feared it was a ghost. Others claimed it was fairy magic. But when the king heard the news, he smiled. At last he had killed poor Snowdrop.

Then one day the wild horse wandered into the palace grounds. The guards, and all the lords and ladies of the court, stood back and gaped in amazement. They had heard of the strange vision, of the sleeping maiden in a glass coffin on a wild horse. But they had not believed it.

They were even more surprised when the king's son ran to the horse and grabbed hold of the glass coffin. Will had recognized his playmate. Weeping, he tried to loosen the coffin to take her from the horse and hold her in his arms.

The king saw that his son still loved the girl. In a rage, he dashed out and pushed the coffin from Will's hands. The glass case shattered upon the ground, and as it fell it so jolted Snowdrop that the piece of poisoned apple fell from her mouth.

She awoke from death as though awakening from a long, long sleep.

Snowdrop told the astonished courtiers all that had happened since she had left the palace. The three robbers were sent for, and they declared that Snowdrop had spoken truly.

Will ordered that the king be punished. The robbers placed magic shoes on the king's feet, and in these he danced and danced and could not stop dancing. He danced far away, never to be seen again.

Meanwhile Snowdrop and Will were married. As queen and king, they ruled the land wisely and well. The banished queen returned to live with them in her old age. And the three robbers gave up their wild ways to live in the palace as Snowdrop's brothers, ready to offer help and advice whenever she needed it.

HAMLET
Ashboy

amlet (1599 – 1601) is Shakespeare's most famous play. It tells of a young Danish prince whose father has died. The father's ghost returns to inform his son that he was poisoned by his brother, who wanted to become king and marry Hamlet's mother. Hamlet is not sure if he can believe the ghost, or if the ghost is real. But he suspects something is wrong, so he pretends he is mad while he finds out if the ghost is telling the truth. When he learns that it is, he seeks revenge. He dies fighting his uncle.

The play is based on a Viking saga, in which the hero is a bit like the stepchild in fairy tales who is badly treated but rises to become a king or queen. Shakespeare

HAMLET

transformed this theme so that it is about the difficult choices people must make in life. In this version, the hero is Ashboy; in the original, he was Amlethi.

Shakespeare may have chosen Hamlet because in English it is easier to say than Amlethi. He may also have chosen it for personal reasons. His son Hamnet had died five years before, when he was only eleven years old. And in the year that Shakespeare wrote *Hamlet*, his own father died.

Hamlet is indeed about the sorrow a son feels for his dead father, but it is also about what goes wrong when people are bad and selfish. Many things seemed to be going wrong in England at that time. Harvests failed, people starved, prices rocketed and jobs were lost. Elizabeth I was very old by then, and people worried about what would happen after her death, fearing they might end up with a bad ruler.

ASHBOY

Long ago, two kings ruled one land. They were brothers, and governed together. Horvendill and Feng they were called. Horvendill had a wife, Gertrood, and together they had a son.

Now everyone thought that the boy was a fool, an idiot. They really believed he was stupid. This was because he was always so quiet and still. His mother laughed at him and his uncle hated him. Only his father, Horvendill, loved the boy. Horvendill knew his son was the quiet type, who loved nothing more than to sit by the fire and watch and think about all he saw and heard.

Even so, "Ashboy, stupid Ashboy!" was what they all called him. He never complained about it — it only made him more shy — and so the name stuck. Everyone forgot his real name, even his father.

Ashboy annoyed his uncle, just by existing. Feng's hatred of Ashboy grew so much that he began to hate his own brother as well. "It's all Horvendill's fault," grumbled Feng, "to have such a stupid boy who so annoys his uncle."

So Feng planned to kill Horvendill. With the help of Gertrood, he would murder his brother.

One misty evening, when Horvendill, Feng and Gertrood were out hunting, Feng shot his brother dead. Later he told everyone in the kingdom that they had become separated. He had tried to catch

up with his brother, but had become lost in the fog. Then, he said, he had heard Gertrood screaming. Thinking she was being attacked, he had run towards her and seen a strange shape in the fog which he shot with his arrow. By mistake, he said, he had killed his own brother.

Feng seemed so upset that the people believed what he said. Shortly afterwards, Feng married Gertrood, saying that now Horvendill was dead he must take care of his wife. But quickly he declared that he and she were to be king and queen, to rule over all the land.

"No one knows the truth!" Feng and Gertrood said to themselves.

Only Ashboy knew what his uncle had done. He, too, had been out wandering that night for he liked the silence of the mist. He had witnessed all that had happened and knew that Feng had murdered Horvendill.

He saw how his mother happily forgot all about his father. He saw how his mother ignored

him. Feng and Gertrood thought Ashboy was no bother to them. He was so stupid, he could never cause them any harm. That's what they thought.

But Ashboy just watched and waited. "I'll survive, and tell on them one day!" he swore. "I'll become a clown. No one will hate me then. When everyone likes me, they'll believe me when I tell the truth!"

He remained in the palace and entertained everyone. Always and every day he performed tricks. Ashboy juggled, he did somersaults and handstands, back flips and cartwheels. Whatever words he spoke were total nonsense. Everyone laughed and said, "What a joker!"

Cruel Feng thought it great fun to tease Ashboy. He would treat the boy as a prince, then make him look more stupid than he really was. One day he invited a princess from a neighboring kingdom to his land. He introduced this lovely young woman to Ashboy and all the people. "This is Ashboy's wife!" he announced. "The two of them shall get married: the idiot clown and the beautiful princess."

Everyone laughed at that. It was a big joke. But Ashboy didn't laugh. Ashboy simply replied, "Uncle, I can't get married, for I've got no brother. If I'm murdered without having a brother, who would my wife marry then?"

People guffawed even louder than before. They thought it was an even bigger joke than Feng's. But Feng and Gertrood didn't laugh. They realized Ashboy knew what had really happened. Suddenly the boy did not seem so stupid, and they feared him.

So Feng contrived to get rid of Ashboy. He called the boy in one day and said, "Ashboy, I'm sorry we made fun of you. Truly, I want you to marry the princess. You are a prince, not a clown. But everyone thinks you're a stupid fool. You must prove to them that you are a prince."

"How do I do that, uncle?" asked Ashboy.

"Go with the princess to her land. Hand over this letter to her father," commanded Feng, giving him a sealed packet. "My neighbor, the king of that country, will read it and do as I say."

"But what did you write?" Ashboy begged to know.

"I have written to tell him that you must prove you are a hero," Feng replied. "I've asked the king to send you on adventures, to fight great battles. When you've done that, you can marry his daughter and become a real prince."

Ashboy took the letter and sailed away with the princess.

Neither knew what the letter truly said. Ashboy

believed his uncle, which proves how innocent he was. But King Feng had lied. What he really wrote was this:

Dear friend and neighbor, take the one who brings you this letter and kill him at once.

As luck would have it, Ashboy's ship got caught in a terrible storm. The ship sank, and only Ashboy and the princess survived. They managed to swim ashore, alive but exhausted. Ashboy fell into a deep sleep and the princess could not wake him. Hearing gruff voices coming towards them, she left Ashboy and ran to hide behind some rocks. She watched to see who the loud voices belonged to.

A band of big, ugly pirates had just landed from their ship. They saw Ashboy and thought he was a drowned man. "Search his pockets!" the pirate captain ordered. "We'll take any money we find. If he's still alive, slit his throat."

The brigands looked through all of his pockets but found nothing on Ashboy except the letter from King Feng. This they tore open and their captain read it aloud. The pirates sighed. One of them felt so sorry for the boy that he started to cry.

"Poor lad," rumbled the cut-throat. "A good-looking young fellow like that shouldn't be killed, especially by such a mean and nasty trick."

It was then that the captain had a brilliant plan. By looking at the seal, they could see the letter was from one king to another. Because pirates don't like kings very much, they decided to play a trick themselves.

Carefully the captain copied the letter, so that in every detail it looked like King Feng's writing. But when he had finished, the letter read:

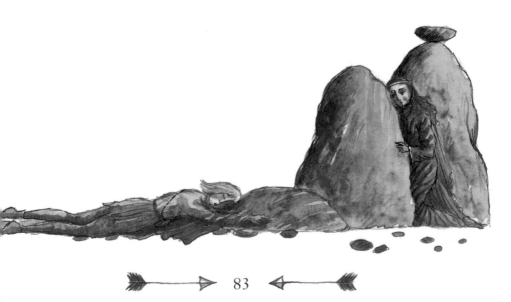

Dear friend and neighbor, take the one who gives you this letter and marry him to your daughter the princess at once.

He carefully folded the new letter and slipped it into Ashboy's pocket. Roaring with laughter, the band of pirates left him sleeping and sailed away.

When Ashboy woke he had no idea of his good luck. But the princess, who had seen and heard all that had happened, came from her hiding place.

"Hurry," she ordered. "We must get to my father's palace as soon as we can."

Together they traveled to her father's palace and Ashboy delivered the letter. He thought the king would send him away at once. He would have great adventures and amazing exploits. He imagined that soon he'd fight giants and destroy dragons. But the only adventure he had was to get married. The king did just as the letter told him to do. Ashboy and the princess were wed at once.

That was a pretty big adventure. The princess was beautiful and he liked her very much.

Now the princess was wise and clever, but she could not let matters lie. She was as chatty and restless as Ashboy was quiet and thoughtful. And she was curious to know why Feng had written such a wicked letter. So she asked her husband, and Ashboy told her all he knew about his father's murder. In return she told Ashboy all she knew — about the pirates, and that his uncle wanted nothing more than to kill him, as he had King Horvendill.

Ashboy wept when he heard this. "What am I to do?" he cried.

The princess soothed him. "Don't worry, my love," she smiled. "I will help you."

Using her wisdom and wealth, her position and power, the princess raised a great army. She called for the finest ships to be built and the best men to be recruited. Together she and Ashboy sailed across the sea with this huge force.

They sailed to the land of King Feng and Queen Gertrood, and they made war. There was banging and blasting and all kinds of bombardment. There was stabbing and slashing. There was great slaughter altogether. The war was so fiercely fought that the green grass turned red with blood and the blue sky turned black with smoke.

But in the end, Ashboy destroyed King Feng. And the princess locked Queen Gertrood in a deep dark dungeon, full of toads and spiders and slimy snakes.

Ashboy and the princess were crowned king and queen of that land. And if they didn't settle down

comfortably, the two of them certainly lived lives of great excitement and wild adventure. But all that's a different story, to be told another time…

KING LEAR
Cap-O-Rushes

ing Lear (1604–5) is about an old king who has three daughters. Lear decides to leave the kingdom to his children. But his youngest daughter, Cordelia, inadvertently angers him and he banishes her. Later, he realizes that the older daughters want only his power and money. They drive him out and, accompanied only by his court jester, he slowly goes mad. Cordelia returns with her new husband and army to fight her sisters. The sisters lose, but by the time Lear and Cordelia find each other again it is too late, for they die soon afterwards.

This play has its roots in one of the oldest and best-loved folk tales in the world. It goes by various

KING LEAR.

names, including "As Much as Salt" and "Cap-O-Rushes." All versions of the tale begin with the king asking his daughters how much they love him. While the play goes on to say what happened to the father, the folk tale follows the fate of the youngest daughter.

Some say Shakespeare got his idea for the play after reading this story in *The Chronicles*, written by Holinshed in 1577. This account has a happy ending, for Cordelia becomes Queen of Britain. Her capital is believed by some to have been the city of Leicester. In fact, that is how Leicester got its name, for it means "the fortress of Lear."

When Shakespeare wrote *King Lear*, his two daughters were in their early twenties and late teens — old enough to marry and leave home. Perhaps he had them in mind when he wrote the play.

CORDELIA

hollow tree in the forest. Then she bathed in the river and made a skirt, a cape and a cap out of the long green rushes that grew at the edge of the water. Dressed like this, she started looking for work. She had to make her way in the world.

The princess went to the castle belonging to the prince of that foreign land. She asked the cook for a job. He didn't like the look of her and said no. But she begged and begged, and finally he relented.

"You can stay to scrub the pots and pans," he sniffed. "All you'll get for it is a place by the fire to sleep, and the scraps of food we don't want."

So it was that the princess found a living scraping pots and pans. In return she was given a place in the ashes to sleep, and the titbits the servants didn't want they threw to her to eat. Because she wore a dress and hat made of rushes, they called her Cap-O-Rushes. Cap-O-Rushes worked in the castle kitchens for a long time.

One day the prince announced that he would hold a festival, to last three days and three nights.

Everyone was invited, rich and poor alike. The servants said the prince was going to choose a wife at the festival. Each serving maid thought he might pick her.

But on the first day of the festival, Cap-O-Rushes said she was too tired to go. The servants left her asleep by the fire. Once she was alone, she ran to the forest and bathed in the river. Cap-O-Rushes put on the first dress that had belonged to her mother. This was a gown made of gold. When she wore it, she shone like the sun in the sky. That is how she went to the festival.

When she entered the great hall where people were feasting and making merry, everyone stopped to stare. They had never seen such beauty. Spell-bound, the prince went up to her and asked her for every dance. Yet Cap-O-Rushes would not tell her name nor from where she came. Before the first day of the festival was over, she was gone. Nobody knew where.

When the servants returned to the kitchens, they found Cap-O-Rushes asleep in her old clothes. No one knew she had been the radiant princess dressed in gold.

On the second day, Cap-O-Rushes was again left alone, sleeping in the ashes. At once she ran to the forest and washed in the river. Dressed in her mother's second gown, which was made of silver, she looked like the glistening moon, skipping and tripping above the clouds.

Just as before, she was the most beautiful woman at the festival. The prince danced only with her. Yet he could not learn her name, nor find out where she lived. Before the day was over, she was gone again. The servants found Cap-O-Rushes sleeping by the fire. They still did not recognize her as the shimmering princess.

On the last day of the festival the servants could not rouse Cap-O-Rushes from her slumber. When she was alone, she ran to the forest and dressed in the third gown, made of gems and jewels. Cap-O-Rushes glittered like the stars. As soon as she arrived, the prince took her by the hand and would not let her go.

"Won't you tell me your name at least?" he implored. But Cap-O-Rushes would not. So the prince took a ring from his finger and put it on Cap-O-Rushes's hand.

"By the ring I will find you and know you, and with this ring I will marry you," he promised.

Cap-O-Rushes smiled. Still she said nothing. She was worried about how she might escape. On this, the final day of the festival, the prince held tightly to her hand and would not let go for an instant.

She feared they would discover she was a kitchen maid, and there would be trouble. But then there was a dance where everyone changed partners. The prince had to let go, and, free at last, Cap-O-Rushes made a dash for the kitchens. She was in her old clothes, asleep, when the other servants returned.

The next day the prince began to search for the woman to whom he had given the ring. But he looked only at grand women — all done up in their finest clothes. He looked at princesses, countesses and duchesses. Never once did he consider ordinary women who worked for a living. So he did not find Cap-O-Rushes.

The prince returned and took to his bed. The doctors announced that he had a broken heart and would die for love.

Everyone said that was a shame — everyone, that is, but Cap-O-Rushes. When she heard the news, she just laughed out loud.

The cook said she was wicked to laugh about the prince dying.

"I laugh because the prince will not die," said the girl. " I could make some soup that will cure him."

"Well then," snorted the cook, "you'd better get on and make it!"

And she did. When the soup was made, and no one was looking, Cap-O-Rushes put the prince's ring into the dish. It was taken to the prince, who drank it. At the bottom of the bowl he found the ring.

"Whoever made the soup must come at once!" he commanded, immediately feeling much better.

The cook feared something must have been wrong with the soup and didn't want Cap-O-Rushes to take the blame for it. He was fond of her and didn't want her to get into trouble. So he went to the prince.

"Who made the soup?" enquired the young man.

"I did, Your Highness," smiled the cook, and bowed deeply.

The cook was a short, fat, balding old man. "Oh no, you can't have made the soup," said the prince. "Send the one who did — I promise no harm will come to her."

The kindly cook went to Cap-O-Rushes and sent her to the prince, saying, "It's no good — he wants you and he's going to get you!"

As soon as Cap-O-Rushes entered the prince's chamber, he asked, "How came you by the ring?"

She looked him in the eye and said, "By him who gave it to me."

Now from the moment she entered the room, the prince knew she was the one to whom he had given the ring. When she saw that he recognized her, Cap-O-Rushes removed her skirt, cape and cap of rushes, showing beneath it her gown of gems and jewels.

As he had promised he asked, "Princess, will you marry me and be my queen?"

And she agreed.

They planned a big wedding. They even invited her father, the wise old king who had asked the foolish question. When Cap-O-Rushes heard he was coming to the wedding, not knowing it was his

own daughter's, she told the cook, "Make the food for my wedding with no salt. Not a handful of salt, not a pinch of salt, not a grain of salt. No salt at all, in fish or flesh or fowl, in pudding or pie or pastry, in soup nor broth, in fruit nor vegetable. No salt at all!"

"That'll taste nasty!" complained the cook.

"It doesn't matter — just do as I say," ordered Cap-O-Rushes.

So the food for the wedding was made without salt. When the guests sat down at the wedding banquet, the food tasted terrible. They all complained, saying, "The wedding is ruined, there's no salt in the food!"

All complained except Cap-O-Rushes's father. The wise old king began to cry. He wept so much that his long white beard was soaked with tears.

The guests all asked, "Why are you crying?"

The old king replied, "Once I had a daughter and I asked how much she loved me. She said she loved me as much as salt, and I thought that meant

she did not love me at all. But now I understand. Without salt, food has no taste. Without love, life has no meaning. My daughter loved me more than all the world, and I've lost her for ever!"

Again he wept. Cap-O-Rushes could bear it no longer. She ran up to her father and put her arms around him. Kissing him tenderly, she said, "Ah, no, dearest father, you have not lost your daughter. Because I am she and I love you still."

The king looked into her eyes and recognized the child he had sent away. He begged her forgiveness, and of course she forgave him. Then she ordered the cook to make fresh food, but this time with salt. The cook went off at once to prepare a new banquet for the guests.

The wedding of Cap-O-Rushes and the prince was such a grand party, such a glorious affair, that it lasted seven years and a day. Each day was better than the one before. And how do I know this? I was at the wedding myself, and that's how I heard the story.

THE WINTER'S TALE
The Flower Princess

The *Winter's Tale* (1610 or 1611) is one of Shakespeare's last plays. It tells of the King of Sicily, who is jealous of his wife, suspecting that his best friend, the King of Bohemia, is in love with her. He fights with his friend and when a daughter is born, insists that he is not the child's father. The queen appears to die of shame, while a faithful servant rescues the baby and takes her to Bohemia. Here, the child is raised by a shepherd and named Perdita. The King of Bohemia's son falls in love with Perdita. This angers his father, who thinks she is not good enough for his boy. The young lovers run away and find themselves in Sicily. By now, the king regrets his actions. When the full story is revealed, everyone is reunited and Perdita's

LEONTES

mother appears again — not dead, but disguised as a statue.

The play is based on a popular book, *Pandosto* or *The Triumph of Time*, by Robert Greene (1588). Woven into Greene's story are elements of many fairy tales, among them the theme of a king and his son who disagree about who the prince should marry. This theme reflected gossip about James I, who was arguing with his son, Prince Henry, about just this problem. Most of Shakespeare's last plays are about fathers and daughters. His elder daughter, Susanna, had married a Puritan and his younger daughter, Judith, was being courted by a man who proved to be untrustworthy. At the same time, Shakespeare's first grandchild was born. With all these family joys and sorrows, maybe it was only natural for Shakespeare to retell stories about fathers and daughters.

PERDITA

KING JAMES I of England

The Flower Princess

There was once a young king of Sicilia who was selfish, restless and hard-hearted. His people wished he would fall in love and settle down. But the king said this would never happen.

Yet one day the king met a young country girl. "You're so beautiful!" he exclaimed.

That she was, and as kind and generous as the king was mean-spirited. His heart softened and he fell in love with her. Before long, the king asked her to be his wife.

The two were married. The new queen was so good that the king changed his ways. He followed her example, and became more like her. People were delighted. "How gentle and kind the king is when he wants to be!" they observed.

After a time, the queen gave birth to a little girl. Everyone rejoiced. The wisest wise woman in the world was invited to the celebrations. She was the queen's best friend, and an oracle — she could foretell the future. On the day the princess was named, many people presented gifts. But the finest came from the wise woman. She gave the girl a golden chain with a pendant in the shape of a flower.

The old woman revealed, "She'll be called Flora, for her joys and sorrows will be among the flowers. Those joys and sorrows will be shared by all who love her."

The King of Sicilia didn't like the sound of this. His daughter was a princess, not a wild girl who roamed among the flowers of the fields and forests. From that time on, he cared nothing for his child.

But the Queen of Sicilia doted on the little girl. The princess got all her attention. The king resented this. He returned to his mean ways, and finally shouted at the queen, "You act like a stupid country woman, fussing over your baby so! We have servants to do that!"

Amazed at these words, the queen quietly replied,

"I am a country woman, and proud of it. And you knew that when you married me. But country woman or queen, I shall always take care of my child and never leave her to fend for herself."

"You will!" roared the king. "Let the princess be left alone, without mother or servants."

In a rage, the King of Sicilia ordered that the child be placed in her cradle, and that the cradle be dropped into the river that ran beside the palace. The order was carried out at once.

Horrified at what her husband had done, the queen fled to the highest tower and locked herself in. She would see no one except the wise woman who had foretold joy and sorrow for her baby, though it seemed the baby's fate was to be all sadness.

"Please let me see you!" the king implored.

No matter how the king begged, his wife wouldn't allow him into the tower. After many days, the wise woman reported, "The queen has died of a broken heart."

When the king heard this he tore his clothes and

covered himself in ashes. Moaning and weeping, he would not be comforted. From that time on, he mourned the loss of his daughter and the death of his wife, all caused by his own pride and anger.

In the meantime, the cradle did not sink. It floated down the river and across the sea. At last it was washed up on the shores of Bohemia, a land far from Sicilia. The cradle tipped the princess on to the sand, and it was there an old man found her.

The old fellow could not think where the child had come from, nor how she had come to be there. There had been no storms, no shipwrecks at all. Even so, he took her home. The old man and his wife had always wished for a child and none had been born to them. "The child is a blessing on us," he decided. "This little girl is the answer to our prayers."

His wife smiled. "Her name's Flora," she announced, "for she wears a golden flower on the chain around her neck."

They raised Flora as their own child. Because they were gardeners, and tended the gardens of the

King of Bohemia, Flora became a gardener, too. She dwelt among flowers every day. Her foster-parents were kind and good. So far, the prophecy had proved to be true: starting life in sorrow, Flora now knew great joy.

Flora grew to be as beautiful and good as her mother once was. Bruno, the Prince of Bohemia, saw her at work in the gardens, and he fell in love with her. Every day as he strolled through the palace grounds he would steal a glance at her. His father did not like this.

"From now on, keep out of the gardens," the King of Bohemia ordered him. "Remain in the palace and stay away from that girl!"

But Bruno disobeyed his father. One day he went to the gardens. When he saw Flora, he wanted more than anything to give her a present, even though he had never even had the nerve to talk to her. So he reached towards a bush to pick a rose.

"Stop!" Flora warned. "Don't touch any flowers on that bush. It's magic!"

Bruno didn't listen, and Flora's warning came too late. As he grasped a rose, a thorn pricked his hand. The prince fell to the ground in a deep sleep.

Flora cried for help and servants carried Bruno to his bed. Doctors were sent for, yet all their pills and potions couldn't cure the careless young man. Prince Bruno slept on and on.

At last the King of Bohemia was so desperate he sent for the wisest wise woman in the world. She was the oracle who had given Flora the golden chain. The old woman declared, "The only cure for Bruno is that he be kissed by Flora and the two get married."

The king didn't like that at all. He wanted his son to be cured, but he did not want the prince to have a mere gardener for a wife. So he plotted and planned. Flora was called, and told to kiss the prince. She happily did so. As soon as their lips touched, Bruno opened his eyes to look around. He was delighted to see Flora.

But the king was ready. "Seize Flora and throw her into the sea!" he cried.

Whether it was because of the direction of the current, or the ebb and flow of the tide, or whether it was the magic of the wisest wise woman, it can't be said. But however it came about, Flora floated across the sea and back to the land of Sicilia, the land of her true father and mother. She was met by the wisest wise woman, who took her at once to the tower where the queen had once hidden.

Meanwhile Bruno's heart was filled with sadness and anger. He screamed at his father, "How could you destroy the only girl I loved? I'll never live in this land, or look at you again until I find her!"

So he set off in search of Flora. For a long time he traveled, until at last the winds brought him to Sicilia. Here the King of Sicilia still ruled. All that time he had sat, miserable and lonely, upon his throne. His clothes were torn and ragged. Ashes and dust covered his body. A pool of tears caused by years of weeping drenched his feet.

His moaning and groaning was echoed by the constant sighing of the lovelorn prince.

"Young man," observed the king, "you seem as sad as me. Tell me why."

Bruno told the king of his search for Flora. Then the king told of his foolishness and anger, and how he had lost both wife and child. The two men wept until the growing pool of tears threatened to drown everyone in the palace.

Then it was that the wise woman appeared. "You stupid idiots!" she cried. "Go to the tower immediately. And for once in your lives, use your brains! Don't speak and don't act before you think."

Amazed, the two men climbed the tower that had for so long been locked. At the top of the tower they found the most wonderful painting. The picture showed two women of great beauty. To the king, the older one looked just like his wife, the Queen. To Bruno, the younger one appeared to be Flora, but in the clothes of a princess, not of a gardener, and still with the flower pendant round her neck.

So shocked were they that the two men did not need to remember to think before they spoke or acted. Instead, they stood like statues. Nothing could have surprised them more than this painting.

But then something even more amazing happened — the painting came to life! The two women in the picture began to move and to sing a song so merry that it dried the men's tears and they laughed more than they had ever done in all their lives.

Then the queen and Flora stepped out of the painting, and ran to put their arms around their loved ones. In all those years, the queen had not been dead but living secretly in the tower, protected by the magic of the oracle. The wise woman had returned Flora to her mother as soon as the princess's feet had touched her native land.

Then Bruno married Flora, and they lived in joy and sorrow — but mostly in joy — from that time onwards.

Sources

The Devil's Bet

Afans'ev, A. N., "The Taming of the Shrew", *Russian Fairy Tales*, trs. Norbert Guterman, George Routledge & Sons, London, 1946.

Bay, J. C., "Bend the Bough in Time", *Danish Folk and Fairy Tales*, Harper and Bros., New York and London, 1899.

Bord, Janet and Colin, *The Enchanted Land: Myths and Legends of Britain's Landscape*, Thorsons, London, 1995.

Briggs, Katharine, "The Watchers at the Well", *A Dictionary of British Folk Tales*, 4 vols, Routledge & Kegan Paul, London, part A, vol. 1, 1970.

Edwards, Richard, *The Waking Man's Dream*, sixteenth century.

Grimm, J. and W., "King Thrushbeard", *The Complete Grimms' Fairy Tales*, Pantheon Books, New York, 1944.

Kennedy, Patrick, "The Haughty Princess", *The Fireside Stories of Ireland*, McGlashon & Gill, Dublin and London, 1870; *Legendary Fiction of the Celts*, Macmillan, London, 1866.

OhOgain, Daithi, "The Bet", or "The Taming of the Shrew", unpublished manuscript, transcript of a field recording in Wicklow Mountains in the 1970s.

The Hill of Roses

Brooke, Arthur, *The Tragicall History of Romeus & Juliet*, 1562.

Garter, Bernard, *The Tragicall & True Historie which Happened between Two English Lovers*, 1563.

MacPherson, George W., "The Stone of Roses", *Traditional Stories of Northwest Skye*, Skye Graphics, Skye, 1984.

Masuccio, Salernitano, *Il Novellino*, 1474.

The Thirty-third Novel of Il Novellino,
trs. Maurice Jones, Davis and Oriolli, London, 1917.

The Novellino of Masuccio, 2 vols,
trs. W. G. Waters, Lawrence & Bullen, London, 1895.

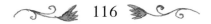

Sources

Painter, William, "The Goodly Hystory of the Love between Rhomeo and Julietta", *Palace of Pleasure*, 1566; also featured in Collier's *Shakespeare's Library*.

Porta, Luigi da, *Istoria novellamente ritrovata di due nobili amanti*, 1535; translated into English by Sir Geoffrey Fenton, 1567.

Xenophon of Ephesus, "The love-adventure of Abrocomas and Anthia", *Ephesiaca* (The Ephesian Story), trs. Paul Turner, Golden Cockerel Press, London, 1957.

A Bargain is a Bargain

Brewer, E. C., *A Dictionary of Miracles, Imitative, Realistic, and Dogmatic, with Illustrations*, Chatto & Windus, London, 1884.

Conway, Moncure David, *The Wandering Jew*, Chatto & Windus, London, 1991.

"Dolopathos and the Seven Wise Men", story originating in the eleventh–thirteenth centuries.

Fiorentino, Giovanni, *Il Pecorone*, circa 1378.

The Novel from which the Play of the Merchant of Venice, written by Shakespeare, is taken, translated by M. Cooper, 1755.

The Pecorone of Ser Giovanni, trs. W. G. Waters, Lawrence & Bullen, London, 1897.

Friedlander, Gerald, *Shakespeare and the Jew*, George Routledge & Sons, London, 1921.

Furnace, Horace Howard (ed.), *The New Variorum Edition of Shakespeare*, J. B. Lippincott Co., Philadelphia and London, 1890.

Gladwin, F., *The Persian Moonshee*, Calcutta, 1795, and London, 1801.

Leti, Gregorio, *Vita di Sisto V*, 1686; printed in English by John Wyatt as *The Biography of Pope Sixtus V*, 1704.

Mahabharata, 200 BC—AD 200, source for an early "bond of flesh" tale, often called the "Dove and the Hawk" story.

Silvayn, Alex, "Of a Jew Who Would for his Debt Have a Pound of Flesh of a Christian", *Orator*, trs. A. Munday, 1598.

"The Story of the Choice of Three Caskets", *Gesta Romanorum* 1340.

Sources

Snowdrop

Briggs, Katharine, "Snow White", *A Dictionary of British Folk Tales*, Routledge & Kegan Paul, London, 1970.

Child, Francis James (ed.), "Rose the Red and Lillie the White", *English and Scottish Ballads*, 8 vols, Little, Brown & Company, and Shepard, Clark and Brown, Boston, 1859.

Garnett, L. M. J. (trs.), "Queen of the Night", *Ottoman Wonder Tales*, A. & C. Black, London, 1915.

Kúnos, Dr Ignácz (trs.), "The Magic Hair Pins", *Forty-four Turkish Fairy Tales*, George Harrap & Company, London, 1913.

Lodge, Thomas, *Rosalynde*, 1592.

Philip, Neil (ed.), "Snow White", *English Fairy Tales*, Penguin Books, Harmondsworth, 1992.

Ashboy

Morley, Henry, *Early Prose Romances*, George Routledge & Sons, London, 1889.

Saxo Grammaticus, *Gesta Danorum*, thirteenth century.

The First Nine Books of the Danish History of Saxo Grammaticus, trs. Oliver Elton, David Nutt, London, 1894.

Thoms, William J., *Early English Prose Poems*, George Routledge & Sons, London, and E. P. Dutton & Co., New York, 1907.

Cap-O-Rushes

Ashe, Geoffrey, *Mythology of the British Isles*, Methuen, London, 1990.

Dougherty, Katherine and Ellen: unpublished transcript of the "Cap-O-Rushes" story collected from my great-aunts.

Folklore Myths and Legends of Britain, Reader's Digest Association, London, 1973.

Geoffrey of Monmouth, *Historia Regum Britanniae*, circa 1136.

—— [Galfridus Monemutensis, pseud.], *Rerum Britannicarum id est Angliae, Scotiae, vicinarumque insularum ac regionum: scriptores vetustiores ac praecipui*, 1587.

History of the Kings of Britain, trs. Sebastian Evans, J. M. Dent and Sons, London, 1963.

The History of the Kings of Britain, trs. Lewis Thorpe, Penguin Books, Harmondsworth, 1966.

Holinshed, Raphael, *Chronicles*, 1577 and 1587.

Perrett, Wilfrid, *The Story of King Lear from Geoffrey of Monmouth to Shakespeare*, Mayer & Müller, Berlin, 1904.

Tatlock, J. S. P., *The Legendary History of Britain*, Medieval Academy of America in association with University of California Press, Berkeley, 1950.

The Flower Princess

Baring-Gould, Sabine, "The Gardener Prince", *Old English Fairy Tales*, Methuen & Company, London, 1895.

Child, Francis James (ed.), "The Gardener", *English and Scottish Ballads*, Folklore Press in association with Pageant Book Company, New York, vol. 3, 1957.

"Patient Grissel", *English and Scottish Ballads*, Little, Brown & Company, and Shepard, Clark and Brown, Boston, 1857.

Greene, Robert, *Pandosto: The Triumph of Time*, 1588; The Shakespeare Library, Gollancz, London, 1907.

Holinshed, Raphael, *Chronicles*, 1577 and 1587.

Lyly, John, *The Woman in the Moon*, 1597.

"The Princely Lovers' Garland", *The Roxburghe Ballads*, number 598, vol. 3, circa 1720.

The Royal Courtly Garland, or Joy After Sorrow, broadsheet ballad, 1790.

Sabie, Francis, *The Fisher-man's Tale and Of the Famouse Actes, Life and Love of Cassander, a Grecian Knight*, 1595.

Flora's Fortune: The Second Part and Finishing of the Fisher-man's Tale, 1595.

Further Reading

There are many interesting books about Shakespeare, his life, the lives of his friends, the way people lived in his day, and, of course, about his plays. Keep your eyes and ears open and you'll find them. And remember — you can always tell a good story more than once!

Barlow, Steve, and Skidmore, Steve, *The Lost Diary of Shakespeare's Ghostwriter*, Collins, London, 1999.

Birch, Beverly, *Shakespeare's Stories*, Macdonald Young Books, Hemel Hempstead, 1998.

Blackwood, Gary, *The Shakespeare Stealer*, O'Brien Press, Dublin, 1999.

Cooper, Susan, *King of Shadows*, The Bodley Head, London, 1999.

Deary, Terry, *10 Best Shakespeare Stories Ever (10 Best Ever)*, Scholastic, London, 2009.

Ganeri, Anita, *What They Don't Tell You About Shakespeare*, Hodder Children's Books, London, 1996.

Garfield, Leon, *Shakespeare's Stories and Shakespeare's Stories II*, Victor Gollancz, London, 1985 and 1999.

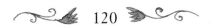